TH̶ ̶OK

*For the moonstruck poet, Gulzar – RS*

*To Giles – DL*

First published in Great Britain in 1999 by Bloomsbury Publishing Plc
38 Soho Square, London W1V 5DF
This paperback edition first published in 2000

Text copyright © Rina Singh 1999
Illustrations copyright © Debbie Lush 1999
The moral right of the author and illustrator has been asserted.

A CIP catalogue record for this book is available from the British Library.
ISBN 0 7475 4795 5 (paperback)
ISBN 0 7475 4112 4 (hardback)

Designed by Dawn Apperley
Printed and bound by Oriental Press, Dubai

1 3 5 7 9 10 8 6 4 2

# Moon Tales

## MYTHS OF THE MOON
## FROM AROUND THE WORLD

Rina Singh and Debbie Lush

BLOOMSBURY
CHILDREN'S
BOOKS

# Introduction

There isn't a place in the world where the moon has not been a cause for wonder, and rightly so. Unlike the sun, which is constant in the sky, the moon is mysterious. It is forever changing and some nights it disappears completely, leaving us in darkness.

Since the beginning of time, people in distant places have looked at the moon and wondered. Why does it only come out at night? Why does it wax and wane? How did it get the marks on its face? Some have worshipped it. Others have tried to steal the heavenly treasure and possess it. In some ancient cultures, the moon was seen as a cold, forsaken place, where people were sent for being bad, and in others it was an enchanted land, a paradise to escape all human woes.

In these stories, moon is a man, a woman, a princess, a sister to the sun and even a mischief-maker. No matter which character the moon plays, it has a central role in these tales, where there is no barrier between the possible and the impossible. These tales of wonder are sacred, because they are attempts of people around the world to understand the moon, its mysterious existence, its intransient nature and its amazing beauty.

Moon tales will lift you to a realm where the mysteries are still alive and the magic of the moon is yours to discover.

**Rina Singh**

# Contents

# The Greedy Man

## CHINESE

In long ago China, in a small village by a river, lived two neighbours. One of them was a kind and generous man. He was a farmer, who tilled the little rice field he had inherited from his father. At night, by the light of the moon, he wove straw baskets to sell in the market. Although he worked very hard, he never managed to have any money left over for extras or to put away for his old age. But that didn't stop him from sharing what little he had with other people in need. He was fondly admired by the villagers for his many kind deeds.

The farmer's neighbour, on the other hand, was cunning and greedy. He made his living as a merchant, riding into town to buy all sorts of provisions, such as tea, salt and fresh fish. When he returned to the village he would sell them to the villagers at a good profit. He'd often lied to the villagers about the true price of some products or the scarcity of others. 'I've heard rumours that there will be no more salt in the market for a few months,' he would tell them most dramatically, after his return from town. Word would spread through the village and people would line up in front of his store and buy all his salt.

Although people in the village didn't care for the merchant, the farmer tried to be friendly with his neighbour. They often did neighbourly things together, such as survey each other's vegetable gardens. Sometimes they had tea together and went on walks on long summer evenings.

One evening, as they were walking along a riverbank, they saw a wounded bird. The little brown sparrow was wet and injured and its little body was throbbing with pain. The kind man stopped to pick it up and stroked its dishevelled feathers.

'Why do you bother with a creature that is half dead? It will be nothing but a nuisance to you,' said the greedy man impatiently. It was beginning to get dark and a new moon was rising. He was hungry for his supper and eager to get home.

'You go on ahead,' said the kind man, gently carrying the bird in the folds of his sleeve. He brought it home and wrapped it up in an old shirt and placed it in a box near the window. He cared for the bird every day and talked to it as if it were a little child. He applied a splint to its broken wing and fed it every day. He became so fond of the bird, the thought of parting with it was painful to him. However, when the bird was well and the wing had healed, he knew he must let it go. One beautiful morning he came out of the house with the bird perched on his hand.

'Go, little one, fly home,' he said, ever so tenderly.

And then a very odd thing happened. The bird spoke.

The kind man was startled to hear the bird say, 'You were so kind to me and you expected nothing in return. I shall come back with a reward for you.' Saying this, the bird flew across the rice paddies.

9

Later that day, the little bird returned with a large pumpkin seed and asked the kind man to plant it. Being simple and trusting, the farmer did as the bird told him. He found a spot in his garden and planted the seed. In a few days, the seed grew into a long vine with many little pumpkins on it. With great delight he watched the pumpkins ripen. When they were ripe, he split open one to eat. It burst, not with pumpkin flesh, but gold. All the pumpkins he cut were filled with riches. The kind man was so thrilled with his good fortune that he rushed to tell his neighbour about it.

'Is that so?' said the greedy fellow to himself. And to make sure his neighbour was not spinning a tall tale, he demanded to see the pumpkins. He walked over to the farmer's house and inspected them carefully. He felt ill with jealousy and was determined to get rich in the same manner.

The very next morning, the merchant went for a walk, looking for a wounded bird. He scoured the riverbank all day before returning home empty-handed. The next day, the merchant even climbed trees, shaking their branches in the hope of finding one helpless bird. On the third day, the merchant came armed with a slingshot. Being impatient and not a very good shot, he missed several times before he hit a bird and broke its wing. The bird fell at his feet and he slipped it into his pocket and brought it home. As he put the wounded bird in a box, he said, 'Here's a deal for you, little bird! I will tend to your wounds every day, if you will get me a pumpkin seed bigger than my neighbour's.' And sure enough, he tended to it every day but made sure to remind it of the reward it owed him.

'Don't forget the seed, little birdie,' he would say every night, as he tucked the bird in the box.

When the bird's wing had healed, the merchant decided it was time to let it go. He took the bird into the garden and held it up to the sky. He was relieved when the bird spoke. The bird promised the merchant that it would come back and he too would get his just reward. True to its word, the bird came back and gave him a pumpkin seed which he planted in a sunny corner of his garden. By day, he would pace up and down his garden, watching for signs of growth. At night, he would gaze at the moon, dreaming of the riches in store for him.

In a few days, the seed grew into a sturdy vine. But instead of lying on the ground as all pumpkin vines must, this one grew towards the skies. Every day it grew higher and higher and it seemed to the

greedy man that it was reaching out to the moon itself. Seeing no fruits on the vine discouraged him and his first thought was that the bird had tricked him. But then his greed got the better of him and he began to get very excited. 'Seems like my reward is going to be greater than my neighbour's. I am destined to collect the gold and silver of the moon, perhaps,' he said to himself, clapping his hands in delight.

The greedy man figured the journey to the moon would take him several days. He packed some rice and noodles and tied a bag to his waist to collect all the riches. He wanted to keep his journey a secret and so he left without saying goodbye to anyone, even his neighbour.

The greedy man began to climb the vine, which did indeed lead to the moon. He climbed and climbed. He must have climbed for several days because when he finally reached the moon he was exhausted. But he didn't stop for a rest. He immediately began searching for the glint of gold and silver. When he found nothing, he beat his head with his fists. He was convinced that the wretched bird had cheated him. 'Wait till I get my hands on that bird!' he shouted. When he looked down at the vine, he was in for another big surprise. The vine below him had vanished. Gone! The entire plant had disappeared. He moaned and groaned and he beat his head some more because he was stranded on the moon.

And there he has lived to this day.

The farmer on earth missed his neighbour. He wondered what could possibly have happened to him. Sometimes, while weaving baskets at night, he would look up at the moon and wonder why there was a man there. And on some nights, when you look up, you too will see a man on the moon. People in China call him the greedy man on the moon.

# The Thieves of Chelm

## JEWISH

Chelm was a very small town, so small that had it been any smaller, it would have been known as a village. Despite its small size, however, the town was famous, famous for the foolishness of its people. It was ruled by a Town Council of Seven Wise Elders who helped solve the town's problems. The problem would be brought before the Elders and they would go into session. They would usually deliberate for seven days and seven nights and come up with a solution so brilliant that it would make people gasp. 'Such a clever way out of this problem could only have been thought of in our Chelm,' they would say, praising their Elders.

Like the time when snow fell over Chelm and made it look so beautiful that people didn't want any footprints on it. So a law was passed that children would no longer walk to school. They would be carried on the shoulders of their parents instead.

And who could forget the year when there was a scarcity of sour cream in Chelm? It had been a dry spring and the cows gave little milk. Pentecost was coming up, a holiday when lots of sour cream is needed to eat with the blintzes. People could not figure out how to get enough sour cream so they brought the matter before the Elders. The Seven Wise Men deliberated for seven days and seven nights and came up with a wonderful idea which became law immediately. Water, which was plentiful in the wells of Chelm, was to be called sour cream and sour cream was to be called water. That way each household would have a barrel full of sour cream. That Pentecost there was no lack of 'sour cream'.

Such was the wisdom of the Elders that the people of Chelm loved them as much as they loved their town. They were truly concerned about improving their town in every way. They organised countless meetings to discuss improvement proposals. Whenever they heard of another town or city having something, they called a meeting to discuss how they could acquire it. After all, what was good for other towns should be good for them too. So you can imagine their excitement when they heard that some towns had street lamps. The streets were actually lit at night. What a bright idea! With street lamps, people would not lose their way on dark moonless nights or stumble on stones they couldn't see or bump into folk they couldn't recognise or constantly apologise for landing on one another. And as was the custom, a meeting was called so the citizens of Chelm could have the opportunity to discuss the idea of

street lamps. The meeting was headed by the Council of Seven Elders, who sat in a row rubbing their foreheads and scratching their beards. Anyone looking at them could see that their brains were hard at work. While the Elders were weighing up their various plans, one of them stood up and said, 'I have an idea!'

'What is it?' they all chorused.

Street lamps, he explained to them, were an expensive proposition for a small town. They would cost them a lot of money. They all nodded in agreement.

'Where will the money come from?' he asked them.

They all looked at each other and became silent. Indeed, where would it come from? It was unthinkable that the money should come out of their funds for the poor, he said. They nodded in agreement again.

He then pointed out that there was this moon in the sky that lit Chelm for half a month and it didn't cost them anything. For the other half it left them in darkness.

'Why don't we steal the moon, my friends, and make it shine for us every night?' said the old man, stroking his beard.

Steal the moon? Steal the moon? The citizens stared at the elderly man in amazement and then looked at each other. What a clever idea! Why hadn't anybody thought of it before? They all gathered around him and revelled in his wisdom as he unfolded the plan. He proposed that they wait for a night when the moon was full and at its brightest. On that night they should steal it and lock it up safely until they needed it.

'A stroke of genius!' cried the people and clapped their hands in approval. They congratulated each other, for only a Chelemite could come up with a plan so brilliant.

Capturing the moon was the simple part of the plan, since there was nobody guarding it. It was the hanging of it that would require some ingenuity. But with so many clever minds, they were not in the least bit concerned. Surely they would come up with a solution to the problem. This was the least of their worries.

So they all waited eagerly for a night when the moon was full and at its brightest. They filled a barrel with water and left it open in the Town Square. Seven strong men were chosen to stand around the barrel. When the moon passed over the barrel, the water shone with its bright light. The men had been waiting for this moment

and quickly covered the barrel with a wooden plank. Then they nailed it down firmly and, to make sure no detail was left unattended, they put the official seal of Chelm on it. Pleased with their handiwork, they moved the barrel into the synagogue and locked it in a room.

After a fortnight, the nights became dark and the Chelemites began losing their way and stumbling on stones they couldn't see and bumping into folks they couldn't recognise and constantly apologising for landing on one another. This was the time! The Elders sent word through the town and the people gathered in the synagogue. Outside the synagogue some clever Chelemites had collected all the ladders of Chelm and were busy tying them together with rope. They were arguing about who would be chosen to hoist the moon in the sky. Inside, the seal was broken by the Elders and the wooden plank removed. All those who were gathered inside expected to be dazzled by the light of the moon. But when the wooden plank was removed there was no moon, just a barrel full of water. The whole town went wild with gossip. They were bewildered. Who would have the nerve to steal their moon, and right from inside the synagogue?

The Elders went into an emergency meeting and after seven days and seven nights they came to a decision. There would be a second attempt to steal the moon and this time they would guard the captured moon more carefully.

And if the town of Chelm still exists, chances are the people are still trying to steal the moon.

# Anansi

## WEST AFRICAN

Long ago in West Africa, Anansi was a spider but he was also a man. When things were hard, when his life was in danger or if there was a famine in the village, he would become a spider – a trickster who was able to overpower all other creatures with his cleverness. But when things were going well, he was a man who lived in a village with his wife, Aso. He had four sons and all of them were strange looking. Anansi would take one look at them and turn away in shame.

'How could you give me sons I'm so ashamed of?' he would ask his wife.

'Anansi! Anansi!' she would scold him. 'They are your sons. You should love them.' Anansi would take one more look at them and shake his head. He was so ashamed, he refused even to name them.

The first one had a mouth so big that when you first looked at him, you thought he had nothing but a mouth on him. You could hardly see his eyes and his nose. His cheeks were pushed up by one enormous mouth stretching from one side of his head to the other.

20

Oh, it pained Anansi even to look at him. The second son had big eyes, as big as sliced pineapples, which popped right out of their sockets too. Every other feature was quite insignificant because his eyes seemed to cover his entire face. The third son was short and fat. It was hard to decide if he was short because he was fat or if he was fat because he was so short. But one thing was clear, he resembled an inflated balloon. The fourth son had an average body above his waist but unusually long legs. So long were his legs that he seemed to walk on stilts. Anansi had to look up as if at the sky to talk to him. Anansi was very disappointed. But Aso, Anansi's wife, raised her sons well. They were polite and hard-working and everyone in the village spoke highly of them. With time, Anansi grew to love them too.

One night, Anansi found a large silver ball in the fields. He had never seen such a beautiful object in his life. It shone so bright that it made the night look like day. A treasure that size could

help buy a farm for each of his sons but it could belong to only one, pondered Anansi. It was a problem he had to solve. Anansi brought a blanket and wrapped the ball in it. He dug a hole in the field and buried the silver ball until he decided what to do with it. He came home and called his sons together.

'Sons,' he said to them. 'We have to go on a journey. I have to find an answer to a very important question. I can't tell you what it is but I want to see which one of you will help me find it.'

So the next day, Anansi and his four sons got ready for the trip and left. They travelled for days and Anansi was sure that there would be a way of finding out which boy deserved the silver ball. Many days passed and there was neither a sign from the skies nor an indication from the earth. It was then that they came to a river. They looked up and they looked down and they saw nothing but the river. There was no boat, not even a piece of wood to float on to cross the river.

'I guess we will have to turn back,' said Anansi. 'There is no way we can cross this river.'

'Wait, Father,' said his first son, stepping forward. 'Let me see what I can do.' He bent down and surveyed the river. Then he opened his enormous mouth and swallowed up the entire river.

'Hee! Hee!' laughed Anansi proudly and they crossed to the other side. Then the first son let the water out.

'Boy, I shall call you Swallow-a-River after that heroic act,' said Anansi. So Swallow-a-River he was called. And they walked until they reached a village. They were tired and decided to spend the night there. Now it so happened that the Chief of the village had lost a jewel of great worth and was offering a bag of gold to anyone who found it.

A bag of gold, estimated Anansi, could easily buy a farm for each of his sons. So they all decided they would try to look for the jewel. They marched to the Chief's house and asked to see him. The Chief came out with his daughter, and Anansi introduced himself and his sons. He offered to find the lost jewel. The Chief took one look at the boys and thought it was a great opportunity to use one of them as a labourer in his fields.

'Anansi,' said the Chief. 'I will make a special deal with you. If you find the jewel within seven days, I'll give you not one but four bags of gold. But if you can't find it then I will keep one of your sons to work in my fields.'

Anansi was outraged at the offer and was about to turn and walk away when

Swallow-a-River, who had fallen in love with the Chief's daughter, spoke.

'Father, that's a good idea. I'll stay behind to work for the Chief till you return.' And so it was agreed. Anansi left with his three sons. For several days they looked and looked but found neither head nor tail of the jewel. On the seventh day, Anansi got very nervous and said to his sons, 'No matter how, we must return to the village and save Swallow-a-River.' And they turned to go back around a mountain when the second son saw something glowing at the top of the mountain. Before Anansi could stop him, he was climbing the mountain and there on the flattened peak was a big red jewel.

'The jewel! The jewel!' he screamed from the top of the mountain. And in his excitement he began waving his arms and lost his balance. He began to fall and hit the mountain sides. The third son saw the danger and knew if he didn't do something

soon, his brother would meet his death on the rocks below.

He took large puffs of air till his fat balloon-like body became even larger and he stationed himself where he thought his brother might fall. And he cushioned his brother as he landed.

'My brave sons!' exclaimed Anansi. 'You will be called Sharp Eyes,' he told his second son. 'For only eyes like yours could spot a jewel so high up on the mountain.' 'And you will be called Save-a-Life because you saved your brother's life,' said Anansi to his third son.

They had found the precious jewel but not in time. It was getting dark and it was still a long way to the village.

'We will never be able to save Swallow-a-River from the Chief's bondage,' lamented Anansi.

'Father,' said the fourth son, 'Why don't I go ahead with the jewel and you catch up later.' Before Anansi had a chance to reply, the fourth son was off, leaping over

mountains with his long legs.

'Oh Lord!' cried Anansi. 'After a performance like that, I'll call him Conquer-a-Mountain.' Anansi and his two sons reached the village later that night and were surprised to find celebrations going on.

The Chief welcomed them and asked them to share in the celebrations.

'Thanks to you and your brave sons I have found my jewel. I will give you the four bags of gold and I will also give my daughter to your son Swallow-a-River in marriage. Do you agree?' Anansi was pleasantly surprised. The girl was pretty. So he agreed and the celebrations lasted many days.

After the celebrations Anansi returned home with his sons and daughter-in-law. He went straight to the fields and dug up the silver ball.

'Look at the treasure, my sons. This was the reason I took you on a journey. I wanted to find out which one of you was most deserving but I found you all deserve it equally. So I'm going to throw it in the air and whoever catches it gets to keep it.'

Anansi took the ball and threw it in the air, as high as he could, and then waited for it to come back. It never did. It went higher and higher and stayed in the sky. It is now called the Moon and there it shines. Anansi's children and their children share equally in its light.

# Hina

## POLYNESIAN

When the moon is full and round and shines brightly over the islands of Hawaii, people look up and say that a woman lives there and her name is Hina. Some believe Hina is a beautiful goddess. Others say she used to live on earth and was the best tapa maker ever. It is true that Hina did not always live on the moon.

In the old days of Hawaii, Hina lived in a cave near the Rainbow Falls. From morning until evening she sat outside her house pounding tapa. Making tapa was not an easy task but she enjoyed turning plain tree bark into beautiful cloth, which she first bleached and then dyed. And then with little wooden stamps, she stamped the cloth with pictures of fish and shells. Hina's tapa was so beautiful that some people in the village stopped making

their own. They only wanted tapa made by Hina. Even the Chief demanded that the tapa for his kites should be made by her. People begged her to make tapa for their special occasions. Sometimes, when they rushed her to make it faster, she would scold them and say, 'Tapa cannot be made faster. It takes its own time.'

Since Hina was a kind person and she could not refuse anyone, she ended up making tapa all day. She chanted as she worked and her chanting could be heard through the valley. Unfortunately, she got no help from her son, Maui, who went from island to island looking for adventures. Her husband, Aikanaka, was even less help. He hunted for wild pigs most of the day and at night came home and complained about everything.

'You are slower than a turtle,' he would tell her. 'Why didn't you make my new

29

cape today?' He was very demanding, and often told Hina to make some Poi, or fetch fresh water from the stream. Sometimes, he would hand her the net to catch shrimp for dinner.

Although she loved making tapa, Hina had grown tired of it. She dreamed of finding a new home where she didn't have to work all the time, where she could enjoy the stars in the night sky, where she could hear the ocean and feel the wind. If only she could find a home where so many things were not forbidden to her such as hunting with her husband or praying with him or eating dinner before she had served him. Then she would enjoy making tapa again, tapa with the colours of the sea and land, the blue of the waves, the pink of the hibiscus and the red of the burning lava.

One beautiful morning, she decided to look for a new home. She rose early and instead of taking her mallet and board out for making tapa, she prayed to her guardian angel, Lauhuki. She prayed for a long time and then waited for some sign from her. She touched the tapa she had made the day before and waited for an image of her new home to appear before her. When nothing happened all morning, she decided to go to the stream and fill the gourds with water for dinner. A light rain began to fall so she hurried to the stream. There she saw colourful reflections in the water. She saw a rainbow that started in the grassy fields and seemed to reach the sun. Hina felt the presence of her guardian angel and thought Lauhuki had answered her prayers. The sun would be her new home. She went to the foot of the rainbow and placed one foot

on it and took a step. She discovered she could walk on it. The rainbow held firm under her feet. With a song in her heart, she threw away the gourds and walked away from the cares of the world. On and on she walked but as she got closer to the sun, her skin began to burn. She got blisters on her feet and she felt dizzy. She fell and slipped back down the rainbow, landing beside her gourds on the grass. When she had recovered, the sun had set and the moon shone on her gently. She felt her strength returning. 'Lauhuki,' she pleaded, 'please show me the way to my new home.'

When she got no answer, she wearily filled the gourds with water and walked back to the cave. Aikanaka filled the entrance of the cave, thundering like a demon.

'Where have you been? Dinner is not even ready and I had to get the water myself,' he said, showing her the gourd angrily.

Hina put down her gourds and went up to her husband. She snatched the gourd from her husband's hands raised it to her lips and had a long drink.

'You evil woman!' shouted Aikanaka. 'How dare you drink water before you have served me dinner?' Hina walked past her husband and went into the cave. She came out with a calabash filled with her most precious things and her tapa mallet and board. Aikanaka blocked her way.

'You can't go anywhere,' he said to her. 'You have not served me dinner. And I want shrimp tonight.' Hina looked disdainfully at her husband, pushed him aside and disappeared into the night.

'Where are you going?' Aikanaka bellowed.

'To my new home!' she called back and hurried towards the stream. There she saw the rainbow glittering with stars. Unafraid of the journey, she said to the rainbow, 'Take me to the moon!'

Aikanaka stared in disbelief as she stepped on to the misty arch. He ran after her but was too heavy for the rainbow. He fell down and grabbed at Hina's ankle. She twisted it free and limped all the way to the moon.

And there she has lived to this day. She is content to watch what she loved on earth: the streams, the volcanoes, the forests and fields. And since then, nobody has made tapa quite like Hina's. The Hawaiians believe Hina still makes tapa on the moon. When it rains, they say she is probably sprinkling it with water. When there is lightning they say she must be shaking the folds out and when they see the clouds they know for sure that she has set out pieces of her tapa to dry.

# The Daughter of the Moon and the Son of the Sun

## SIBERIAN

One day, as Sun was about to retire for the night after a busy day, his son Peivalke came up to him and said that he wished to get married. 'Have you chosen a bride for yourself?' asked Sun. Peivalke told his father that he had tried the golden boots on the maidens of the earth but their feet were too heavy and none of them could follow him into the sky. Sun suddenly remembered that Moon had recently given birth to a daughter. He promised his son that he would speak to Moon. Sun had to admit that Moon was quite pretty and he hoped her daughter had taken after her.

The next day, Sun rose early just before Moon was about to take her rest and proposed to her. 'I hear you have a daughter,' said Sun. 'You are very fortunate indeed because I have found a husband for her. He is none other than my own son, Peivalke.'

Moon was aghast. 'But my daughter is only an infant. She is lighter than my lightest beam. How can your mighty son marry my daughter?' she asked nervously.

The arrogant Sun waved her worries aside. 'In my bountiful household your daughter will be nourished well and will soon grow strong,' said Sun.

'Your Peivalke will scorch my little daughter,' protested Moon. 'And moreover, she is betrothed to Nainas of the Northern Lights.'

'Aha, so that's it! You reject my wonderful son, my only child, for that miserable Nainas,' thundered Sun angrily. 'My Peivalke will wed your daughter if he so wants,' threatened Sun. And to impress upon Moon his strength, he let the thunder roll. He caused ocean waves to lash out in rage and he made the winds howl. The frightened Moon hurried away. She went home and clutched her daughter to her

bosom, whilst trying to think of how to keep her safe from Sun's fury.

She looked down on earth and saw a village near an icy lake in the North. There she saw an old childless couple who looked like kind people and she decided to hide her daughter with them. Sun and his Peivalke could search the skies but they would never find her daughter. She put her in a beautiful wooden cradle and left her in front of the couple's log cabin. They had just settled by the fire for the evening when they were startled by a child's cries outside. Together they went out to look and they discovered a wooden cradle. To their delight, they found in it a beautiful baby girl, bright as a moonbeam. They brought the cradle inside, hardly believing their good fortune, and raised the girl as their own daughter. And because she cried, 'Niekia, Niekia' whenever she played, they named her Niekia.

As the years passed, Niekia grew into a beautiful young woman with silver plaits reaching her waist. She helped the old man collect wood in the forest and from the old woman she learned how to make quilts with reindeer hide and embroider them with beads.

Word travelled and reached Sun that there was an unusually pretty maiden living in a village near an icy lake in the North. He quickly summoned Peivalke and told him to seek her out and marry her if he liked her. Peivalke came down to earth and the moment he set eyes on Niekia, he knew she was Moon's daughter. She looked so much like her mother. He was so charmed, he wanted to marry her right away. But first she had to try on the golden boots. Niekia was on her way to the forest to collect some wood when Peivalke stopped her and asked her to try on the golden

boots. Not knowing any better, she put her feet in them and cried out, 'Ahh, they burn me!'

'Never mind,' said Peivalke. 'You will get used to them when you marry me and live in the sky, for I am Peivalke.' Niekia suddenly realised that he was the son of Sun. It was to escape this villain that she had been forced to separate from her mother.

'Marry you? Never!' cried Niekia, kicking off the shoes. She ran as quickly as she could and hid in the forest until the day was spent. As Moon rose in the sky she followed its beams and came to

40

a deserted cabin.

She entered the cabin and noticed how untidy it was. She began cleaning and putting things in order. When she had finished, she fell asleep in a corner. She was awakened by heavy footsteps and saw silver-clad warriors, each more handsome than the other. They were the Northern Lights brothers and her eyes fell on Nainas, the one to whom she was betrothed, the one she watched every night in the sky. Nainas looked around at their clean cabin and was sure a woman had cleaned it.

'Please show yourself,' said Nainas, because he felt a woman's presence in the cabin.

'If you are old, you will be like a mother to us and if you are not so old, you will be a sister and if you are young, you will be a bride for one of us.'

Niekia shyly presented herself and, like Peivalke, Nainas recognised her because she looked like Moon.

'You are more beautiful than I imagined,' he told her. They were delighted to find each other. Niekia found out that every evening the brothers came to the cabin. They had mock battles among themselves with their silver swords, making spectacular flashes and sparks in the sky. They played games, rested and before Sun rose, they flew away. Every morning Nainas would tell Niekia to wait for him and then fly away. One day Niekia begged Nainas to stay because she missed him when he was gone. Sun would pierce him with his fire and kill him, he explained to her. Niekia thought of a

plan to keep him in the cabin for one day. She secretly made a quilt of reindeer hide and embroidered stars on it with silver beads. Before the brothers came back one night, she hung the quilt on the ceiling over the bed where Nainas slept and covered all the windows. That evening the Northern Lights brothers came, had their mock battles, played games and fell asleep. In the morning, Nainas woke several times but seeing the stars still in the sky, he thought it was too early to rise. Later in the morning, Niekia went to the forest to collect some wood and shut the door lightly behind her. Nainas and his brothers would have slept the whole day, had the wind not opened the door and had they not seen Sun shining through the door. Nainas grabbed his armour and dashed out, calling his brothers. Sun saw Nainas and recognised him as the rogue who had deprived his son of a bride. He saw this as an opportunity to take revenge. He pierced him with his fire and pinned him to the ground. Niekia, who was coming back from the forest, realised too late what she had done. She ran towards Nainas and threw herself on him to shield him from Sun's fire. 'Quick, fly away,' she whispered to Nainas and let him escape to safety. Sun seized Niekia by her silver plaits and was about to toss her up to the sky when he suddenly remembered that his son was still without a bride. He sent a messenger to summon Peivalke. Now was a good time to have a wedding, thought the infuriated Sun. And he would have his revenge too. When Peivalke arrived, Sun said to him, 'Here is your bride. Marry her.'

'You may burn me to ashes but I will never marry your son,' said Niekia bravely.

This maddened Sun even more. He caught hold of Niekia's plaits again and flung her up into the sky, where Moon caught her and held her in her arms. And there she is still today. Niekia's shadow is still on Moon's face as she looks at the Northern Lights and watches Nainas with longing as he engages in spectacular battles in the night sky.

# The Rabbit and the Moon Man

## CANADIAN

A Rabbit once lived deep in the Canadian forest. He lived with his old grandmother in the thickest part of the forest, where the maple and the pine trees kept icy winds from reaching in with all their might. Rabbit was a great hunter and all day he busied himself with laying snares and setting traps to catch little animals and birds. He was quite pleased with himself for being able to hunt daily and provide squirrels, mice and little birds for his grandmother and himself.

One day in winter, Rabbit noticed that his snares were empty. And for some weeks after that they remained empty. Rabbit began to worry. After much investigation, he came to the conclusion that someone was stealing from his traps. He saw tracks all around him, which was a sure indication that animals were prowling about in that part of the forest. He knew he was being robbed. He told his grandmother that he would rise early in the morning to check his traps.

The next morning, Rabbit rose just as the sun was rising and went to see his traps. They were empty. Rabbit couldn't understand what was happening. He decided to rise even earlier the next day. The sun had barely touched the horizon with its first light and Rabbit was up to check his traps. To his great surprise, the traps were empty. The thief was proving to be cleverer than him, but Rabbit was not about to give up. He went back to his burrow and told his grandmother, 'Now I will rise even earlier and catch the thief who is robbing us of our game.'

The next day, Rabbit rose in near darkness and hurried to his traps. He was sure he would beat the thief this time. But he was horrified to find the traps empty again. Morning after morning, Rabbit rose hungry and cold and hurried to the traps only to find them empty.

At last, one morning after a fresh snowfall, Rabbit discovered the marks of a long

foot near his traps.  He was sure that they were the marks of the thief who was stealing his game so stealthily.  He examined the footprints very carefully.  They were long and narrow and extremely light.  Rabbit was puzzled.  He had never seen tracks like that before.  And Rabbit, though a little frightened, was determined to catch the culprit. He went to his grandmother and told her about the strange footprints near his traps and said to her, 'Now I will rise even earlier and retrieve my game before the robber gets there.'  Although Rabbit's grandmother worried for his safety, she didn't want the thief getting away with it.

The next morning and every morning after it, Rabbit rose early, as early as he could, but the man with the long foot was always there before him.  No matter how early Rabbit rose, he was always late and his traps remained empty.  So Rabbit came up with a plan and he told his grandmother about it.

'The robber is always there before me,' he said.  'I will make a snare for him with a bowstring and I will wait all night for him.'

So Rabbit set to work.  He made a snare with a bowstring and set it beside his

traps. He took the other end of the bowstring to a clump of maple trees a little further away and hid behind one of the trees. Rabbit hoped that the thief would step into the snare set for him and he would pull the bowstring, drag the thief and tie him to the tree.

It was a crisp and chilly night when Rabbit came to keep a vigil. The moon was there and stars glittered in a clear cold sky. Rabbit waited, his whiskers twitching nervously. Suddenly it became dark, so dark he couldn't see himself for a while. Rabbit looked up and the moon was gone. The stars were still there. And it was very strange because there were no clouds for the moon to hide behind. Rabbit fidgeted with fright but he decided to wait. Then he saw someone coming. He saw a body of white light sneaking through the trees. The light dazzled him. It headed towards his traps and there it paused, looking everywhere like a thief would. Rabbit pulled the bowstring, closed the traps, dragged the thief and tied him to the tree. He saw the thief struggling to free himself. Rabbit knew he had captured his enemy but he was too frightened to do anything so he ran to his grandmother.

'I have captured the thief,' he told his grandmother. 'But I'm too frightened. His light is too fierce.'

'You must go back,' advised his grandmother. 'Tell him he should stop stealing your game.'

'I will go in the daylight. Maybe I should get some sleep,' said Rabbit.

But his grandmother insisted that he go right away. So Rabbit went and approached his traps. The light was still there. It was so bright, it nearly blinded him. As he came nearer, his eyes became sore and itchy. He went to a nearby stream and washed his eyes with icy water. But the light must have damaged his eyes because he couldn't stop blinking and tears flowed. Rabbit had an idea. He scooped up little balls of snow and threw them at the light, thinking they would put it out. Instead, the snowballs melted the moment they touched the light. Rabbit was enraged.

'The villain,' he said to himself. 'Does he hope to get away with this?'

Rabbit dug in the snow. Under the snow, under the bed of fallen leaves, was cold, black mud. He made balls of the mud and threw them at the light with all his force.

'Stop that!' screamed the prisoner. 'And why have you tied me? I am the Moon Man and I must go back before the sun rises. Untie me or I shall kill you.'

Poor Rabbit shook with fright and ran as quickly as he could to his grandmother and told her what had happened.

'Oh dear!' exclaimed his grandmother. 'No good can come out of this. He will kill us all. Run, Rabbit, run. Release him before the day breaks.'

So Rabbit, even more frightened than before, went back.

From a distance Rabbit cried, 'I will untie you, Moon Man, but you must promise never to rob my snares.'

'I promise, I promise,' said the Moon Man desperately. 'Now let me go before the night is spent.'

Rabbit had to blink his eyes to reach the light and as he came nearer, his shoulders burned, but he quickly cut the snare with his teeth and the Moon Man hurried away. He was in such a hurry, he didn't even look back. And since then, Rabbit blinks all the time and the Moon Man has kept his promise and has never returned to earth. He does his work in the sky, lighting the forest by night, and for a few days every month, he goes away to wash off the mud but he never succeeds. He comes back to shine on the forest but carries the mud marks and will probably do so for ever.

51

# The Sun, Wind and the Moon

## INDIAN

Moon was the youngest of Star Mother's three children. Her two brothers, Sun and Wind, were much older and very abrupt in their manner. Sun, for instance, was constantly chasing Moon out of the sky and when Star Mother scolded him for being bad, he secretly sneered at her for being so dim. And he never tired of showing off his own light and reminding Moon how pale she was in comparison. Wind, on the other hand, loved teasing his little sister. Pushing clouds in her face to cause confusion was his favourite occupation. Bullied by her brothers, Moon felt unloved and lived unhappily in the skies, where exciting things rarely happened. So it was quite an occasion when Thunder and Lightning announced a feast.

A grand feast it was to be, for nothing that Thunder and Lightning ever did was quiet. And now that they had decided to get married, the entire kingdom of the skies filled with their roars and resounded with their rejoicing.

Word spread through air, on earth and under water that there was to be a grand celebration. Because Thunder and Lightning had to invite creatures of the earth and the ocean, the feast was to be held where sky and earth meet.

The preparation for the celebration began days in advance. The most excited were the winged creatures, who were kept busy bringing delicacies from faraway lands. The parrots went on long journeys to bring special berries from enchanted forests. Bees gathered nectar from royal gardens. The stronger birds, such as the eagles, soared to faraway groves to pick the ripest of mangoes and the reddest of pomegranates. The peacocks rehearsed dances that would show off their splendid feathers. The ocean promised to provide music.

A guest list was drawn up and of course Moon's name was on it. Thunder and Lightning were both charmed by Moon's gentle yet startling

beauty but were not particularly fond of her brothers, Sun and Wind. Sun, they thought, was rather arrogant, flashing his light everywhere with no consideration for others. And Wind was so rough in his ways, pushing and shoving anyone who came in his way. But they reluctantly added the names of Sun and Wind to their list because they didn't want to offend old Star Mother. In fact, so rough were Sun and Wind in their ways that when they received the invitation they ridiculed Moon.

'Why would anyone want to invite a weakling like you to a feast?' asked Sun.

'Maybe they didn't want to hurt her feelings,' laughed Wind, pushing a cloud in his sister's face. Sun laughed with his brother. After much speculation they came to the conclusion that Moon was invited because of them and they warned her to behave herself at the feast.

Moon, hurt by such insensitive comments, went to her Star Mother and cried, 'I don't want to go. I'll only be miserable there. I don't wish to go with brothers who bully me.' But Star Mother insisted that Sun, Wind and Moon all go to the celebration together, as one family. And they did.

On the day of the feast, the sky was lit up every which way. Stars were shooting from one end to another. A light breeze carried the many scents of blossoming trees, bushes, herbs and grasses from the surrounding jungles. The first of the guests began to arrive, laden with gifts and treasures. Dawn came and spread her radiance everywhere. The fish leaped in and out of crystal blue waters. The oysters brought gifts of pearls so white. The Rainbow arched gloriously into the feast, bringing the most amazing colours which made the guests gasp with wonder. The clouds gave rides to butterflies, who seemed to be the most excited of all. The guests were enchanted by the beauty of Moon and basked in her silvery radiance. The birds sprinkled jasmine petals everywhere. The tigers roared, the nightingales sang and peacocks danced, captivating everyone with their feathers.

Squeaks and whistles filled the air. What a wedding it was!

There was feasting and rejoicing and great merriment. They all had a wonderful time and after a while even Moon began to enjoy herself.

When the feast was over, Sun, Wind and Moon went home. Star Mother, who had spent her time waiting for her children, looked at Sun and asked eagerly if he had brought back anything for her. Sun rebuked his mother for being so childish.

'I went to enjoy myself, Mother, not to bring back things for you. I did bring back some food but it's for me,' said Sun and, turning his back, he continued to feast on the leftovers he had brought with him.

Star Mother then looked at Wind.

'What about you, Wind? Did you remember your mother?'

'Oh, Mother,' said Wind impatiently. 'You not only behave like a child but you are so unreasonable too. Why don't you just go to sleep?' Saying no more, he turned his back on her too.

Disappointed, Star Mother then looked at her Moon. Before she could even say anything, Moon smiled and unfurled some of the berries and fruits she had brought back with her. Star Mother had tears in her eyes.

She looked at Sun and said, 'Because you thought only of yourself and you turned your back on me, people on earth will turn their backs on you. In summer, you will burn in your own heat and people will wish you would go away.'

And to Wind she said, 'For being so rude to me, your very breath in the hot days of summer will shrivel things up and in winter people will shut their doors on your face.'

And to her little daughter she said, 'My little Moon, you thought of your mother amidst your pleasure. For that your rays will fall softly on earth and people will sing praises to you. You and your beauty will forever remain a mystery to the world.'

And so it has been to this day. The people in India stay away from the sun and wind, but the moon is loved by all.

# The Buried Moon

## ENGLISH

Long ago, Cars in Lincolnshire was marshland.  To walk through the marshes on a dark night was giving an invitation to death.  But on moonlit nights it was safe to walk through them, nearly as safe as it was to walk in the day.

On dark moonless nights, the Dead Things, the Creepy Things, the Bogles and every Crawling Horror came out and attacked anyone who was foolish enough to wander through the marshes.

When the Moon heard about what was going on when her back was turned, she was greatly disturbed.  She decided to probe into the matter herself.

One night, when she was supposed to be resting, she wrapped her black cloak around her, pulling up the hood to cover all her shining hair.  She stepped on earth with only the light from her shining feet to guide her.  She walked to the bogs on a rainy night, stepping along tussocks of grass, in pools of dark water, pushing aside branches all twisted and bent.  Dark shapes leaped from behind the trees.  Around her, the Witches rode on brooms, the eyes of their cats gleaming.  Shrieks erupted from

58

the waters all around. Moon trembled and pulled her cloak tighter around her, but she wanted to see all that had to be seen. So she went from one murky waterhole to another till she tripped on a stone, fell and twisted her ankle. She nearly cried out aloud in pain. The howling wind got stronger and rain beat down on her viciously. She looked around for something to hold on to, caught hold of a branch and tried to steady herself. In a flash, the branch had wrapped itself around her wrists and held her prisoner. Moon pulled, twisted and struggled to break free but it held her fast. She knelt there trembling for her life, wondering if anyone would pass that way and help her. And when she looked around at the forlorn marshes, she had her answer. Who in their right minds would dare to venture out in a place so deadly, on a night so horrifying? As Moon was thinking what to do, she was startled by a human cry that pierced the wet night. She looked around and with the little light from her shining feet, she saw a man being dragged away by Goblins, from the path that led out of the bogs. The imprisoned Moon was furious and she struggled even more to free herself so she could help the man. As she struggled harder, her hood fell back and light streamed from her shining silver hair. The bogs were lit, the sounds of the wind began to fade and it stopped raining. The Creeping Horrors and the Evil Things screamed in panic and crawled back into their corners because they couldn't stand the light. The terrified man cried with joy because he could see the path. He was in such a hurry to escape that he never looked back at the wonderful light that saved his life.

Moon was happy that the man was safe at last and for a moment she forgot she needed help herself. She wished she could be free too so she struggled some more. She twisted and she pulled. In the futile struggle, her hood covered her head again

and it became dark once more.

And with the darkness came back the Howling and Screeching Things. Dark shapes exploded all around. They now knew that Moon was trapped in their marshes and they crowded around her. They kicked her and abused her, all the while mocking her, for she was an old enemy of theirs. Moon felt as if her legs were rooted to the ground and her throat were paralysed. She cringed while an argument went on among the Evil Things about how best to punish their enemy.

'Why don't we poison her?' cackled one Witch.

'Poison her! Poison her!' cackled all the Witches in approval. And the Evil Things howled with laughter.

'No, let's choke her!' screamed a Crawling Horror.

'Choke her! Choke her!' screamed all the Crawling Horrors. And the Evil Things roared with laughter.

'Strangle her!' snarled a Bogle.

'Strangle her! Strangle her!' echoed all the Bogles.

And the Evil Things bellowed with laughter. They stood around Moon, cursing her and shouting at her. Moon flinched and wished she were dead. And this went on most of the night. They fought and argued about how best to punish Moon until someone noticed the grey light in the sky and they knew there wouldn't be enough time to execute a decision even if they came to one. So they grabbed Moon and pushed her into a bog. Then they searched for a big,

heavy stone and laid it on her to stop her from rising. And there Moon lay trapped beneath the stone, hidden from sight.

Days passed and the time came for the New Moon. The marsh folk were happy and looked forward to her coming. Moon was a good friend to them. She made their paths safe again. But the time of the New Moon came and went and there was no sign of her. Days and nights passed and Moon never came. The Evil Things became worse than ever. They left the bogs and came into the streets. The people were afraid to leave their homes at night. When they heard the Evil Things pacing their porches, the townspeople were afraid to turn out their lights for fear they might cross their thresholds and invade their homes. At night they huddled together by firesides praying for Moon to come back.

When the people could bear it no longer, they got together and went to the Wise Woman who lived in the Old Mill and asked her if she knew where Moon was. She read her books and looked into mirrors and her brewpot but she could not tell where Moon was. Instead she told them to keep a pinch of salt, a button and some straw at their doorsteps to ward off the Evil Horrors. They went away disappointed and wherever they gathered, whether it was in the street or at the inn, the townspeople talked of nothing else but the missing Moon.

Days passed and one day at the inn

a man shouted, 'I know where Moon is!'  So everybody at the inn gathered around him to hear his story.

'What a fool I've been,' he lamented.  'I know where Moon is and I didn't realise it until now.  I was so amazed by the experience that I just forgot.'  Then he told them how one night he had been lost in the bogs and how Moon had saved his life.  So they all went back to the Wise Woman and told her what had happened.  The Wise Woman looked at her books again.  She peered into her brewpot and she saw a light.  She told the people to go into the bogs before nightfall, with stones in their mouths, for they must not speak, and with hazel twigs in their hands to keep the Evil Things from getting too close.  She told them to stay together and keep walking till they saw a coffin, a cross and a light.  There, they would find Moon.

The men and women huddled together and walked to the bogs with stones in their mouths and hazel twigs in their hands. The Evil Things screeched and howled, some daring to touch them with their cold, wet fingers, but the people walked on saying nothing till they came to a stone that resembled a coffin. On it they saw a cross of dried twigs and a light shining out from under the stone. They stopped there and said their prayers. They crossed themselves and then together they lifted the stone, stepping back in total amazement, for a shining light that nearly blinded them blazed out. The dazzling light made them squint, but before they knew what was happening, it was in the heavens shining down on them. Moon had escaped to safety and was thankful to the marsh folk for rescuing her. She has remained grateful ever since and shines her brightest over the deadly bogs where she was once buried.

# The Moon Princess

## JAPANESE

In a little cottage at the edge of a village near Mount Fujiyama lived an old woodsman with his wife. Every morning, the old man went off to cut bamboo in a forest at the foot of the great mountain, while his wife stayed at home and looked after their cottage. They would have been content with their lives, had it not been for their constant regret that the gods had not given them any children. On warm summer mornings, the old woman would sweep out the yard and think how nice it would be to have a little girl sitting on the steps, playing with dolls. And every time the old man went into the forest to cut bamboo, he pretended his son was trailing behind him and he talked to him softly, pointing out the wonders of the forest.

The children of the village often followed the old man as he walked to the forest. They teasingly called him 'Grandpa' and begged him to bring back bamboo sticks for them. 'I will give you bamboo if you come and live with me,' the old man would say. On hearing this, the children would run away screaming.

One evening, the woodsman came home and cried to his wife, 'Why were we never blessed with a child?'

'It was not meant to be,' answered his wife. That night, they both prayed to the spirit of Mount Fujiyama, begging to be blessed with a child, and cried themselves to sleep.

A few mornings later, the woodsman walked towards the forest, and strangely no children followed him. His spirits were low and his mind was blank and all day he cut bamboo listlessly. Slowly the moon rose over the forest and it was time to go home. The bamboo he was cutting was young and green with a hollow centre and he knew that with a few more cuts it would be down and he would have finished his work. No sooner had it fallen, than the inside of the hollow bamboo burst with light. The astonished woodsman trembled with fear at first and then looked into the hollow centre of the bamboo. He saw a tiny girl, the size of his thumb, of such dazzling beauty that he had to shade his eyes against the light radiated by the tiny figure. He

64

gently picked up the tiny girl and hid her in his kimono. This was miraculous, the woodsman thought repeatedly, as he headed home to break the news to his wife.

'Bring a basket and a blanket and hurry,' said the old man to his wife, as he entered the yard. The old woman thought her husband had lost his wits. He came home without any bamboo and then he asked for a basket and a blanket.

'What for?' asked his wife, still standing there.

'Don't ask any questions. Hurry up and I'll show you a miracle!' said the old man excitedly. When his wife had put the basket and blanket in front of him, he carefully took out the bamboo child from his kimono and placed her in the basket.

When the woodsman told his wife the story, they both wept with joy, for the great spirit of Mount Fujiyama had sent them a child to keep.

Wherever they placed the basket in the house there was a strange radiance around it. She must surely be a princess, they said to themselves, for a child so fair and beautiful could only be of royal birth. They named her Princess Kaguya. The next day the woodsman returned to collect his bamboo and to his amazement he found gold and silver in the hollow of the bamboos he had cut. He was greatly puzzled by what was happening in his life so he went to a wise scholar who lived nearby and told him his story. The wisdom of the scholar was such, and his experiences so many, that nothing surprised him. He listened to the story with great interest and agreed that the woodsman had done the right thing in hiding his good fortune. He advised the woodsman to keep the whole thing a secret in order to avoid gossip in the village. So the old man and his wife raised the child in secret, and she grew accustomed to staying indoors and didn't seem to mind. The old man didn't need to cut as much bamboo as before because the gold and silver he collected from the forest enabled them to live a comfortable life.

Many years passed and the child grew into a beautiful maiden. Neighbours who caught glimpses of a beautiful girl in the window began to talk among themselves. They noticed how comfortably the couple lived without working as hard and concluded that an emperor's daughter was taking refuge in the house of the old couple. Rumours spread far and wide of her beauty and sons of royal families came seeking her hand in marriage.

'I have no wish to marry,' Princess Kaguya told her parents and refused every suitor who came to their door. The old couple worried for their daughter and tried to reason with her. 'We are getting old and as much as we want you with us, we would like to see you get married and have a home of your own. At least have a look at the

young men.  Maybe one of them will be a worthy husband for you.'

'I cannot marry,' she said to them.  Then, seeing the grief she had caused her parents, she agreed conditionally.  She would marry anyone who could complete the task she set for them.  For instance, she asked one prince to bring a jewelled branch from a tree growing on the sacred mountain.  And she asked another prince to bring a colourful ball lying in the throat of the mountain dragon.  From another prince she wanted a cowrie shell hidden inside a bird's stomach and the prince was not to harm the creature even if he found the right one.  The tasks she set for them were so impossible that they all failed.  The news of Kaguya's beauty and her failed suitors reached the Emperor, who became curious and wanted to see her.  He sent a messenger to the old man's house with an invitation for his daughter to appear in the royal court.  The old man was overjoyed but the invitation left his daughter unmoved.

'Please tell the Emperor I cannot go,' she said, dismissing the requests of her father. The Emperor was at first annoyed that the daughter of a mere bamboo cutter would dare refuse his invitation but then he became even more curious.  He made one more attempt, summoning the old woodsman and promising him a great reward if he succeeded in persuading his daughter to see him.  The woodsman returned and begged his daughter not to miss the chance to become an empress.

'Please, Father,' she implored.  'Do not force me to do anything against my will. Even if I wanted to marry him I couldn't.'

The persistent Emperor decided to visit the old man's cottage himself.  One day, he arrived unannounced and, dismissing all ceremony, walked right into the house. When he saw the exquisite form of the old man's daughter, he fell in love with her.

She sat quietly on a mat, her hands folded in her lap with great dignity. Her black hair fell over her shoulders, reaching the mat she was sitting on. 'Marry me, please marry me,' he pleaded.

'It's not possible. There will be nothing but grief for you,' she said helplessly. 'Please go away.'

The Emperor left in a daze and continued to woo her for many months without any success.

Four years passed and a strange mood settled on Kaguya. Night after night she sat by her window and gazed up at the moon. She looked so unhappy that the old couple started to worry about her, especially the old woman, who knew that bad things happened to moon gazers. When they told Kaguya their fears, she isolated herself even more and remained behind shut doors.

'What is the matter with you?' they begged her to tell them.

'There is a secret I can no longer keep,' she said to them, weeping. 'I am the Princess of the Moon and the time has come for me to go back to my home. My Moon mother sent me to earth to escape a danger that no longer exists. And now I must go back to my people.' The old couple were besides themselves with grief.

'You cannot leave us. We have loved you as a daughter,' cried the woman.

'When the August moon is full I will have to go.'

August came and night after night the moon grew rounder and fuller. The

woodsman panicked. He told his wife not to let go of their daughter's hand while he went to seek help from the Emperor, who was amazed by his miraculous tale. He promised to dispatch hundreds of samurai on the fateful night, to fight the warriors of the moon, and secretly hoped to wed the Princess. The evening of the full moon arrived and the samurai cleverly hid themselves around the woodsman's cottage. Inside the cottage, the Princess of the Moon cried softly with her head on her earth mother's lap. 'I will never forget the love and devotion you have shown me. Try to remember our happy years together,' she consoled her mother.

As the August moon reached its zenith, an unearthly light, one hundred times brighter than the sun, filled the sky and the blinded samurai crouched in terror. A single moonbeam came down and lifted up the princess, who wept all the way to the moon. It is believed in Japan that her silver tears took wing and became fireflies, and on moonlit nights her tears can still be seen. Those who have not heard the tale still call them fireflies, not knowing that they are the tears of the Moon Princess who still cries for those she loved and left behind on earth.

# Why the Moon Waxes and Wanes

## AUSTRALIAN

In Dreamtime, all animals, reptiles and birds, and the sun, the moon and the stars were men and women. They could change into human form whenever they so wished. In Dreamtime, when the spirits freely roamed the earth, Bahloo the Moon lived in the skies. He still lives in the skies but he waxes and he wanes. He changes his shape all the time. Back then he was always round and bright. He lived by himself and at times felt very lonely. He looked upon the maidens of earth and longed to have a wife as a companion, someone he could talk to, someone he could take along on his long journeys across the skies.

Many times he went to places where campfires were lit and he begged the girls to come with him.

'Marry me, please marry me,' he would say to them and the girls would run away into their huts. Whenever Moon tried to enter a group, the elders would see him coming from a distance and they would tell all the girls to go and hide.

Moon's persistent search for a bride became a nuisance to many tribes. The elders warned their young women to stay away from the very light of the Moon.

One night, Bahloo the Moon looked down on earth, which was softly lit by his own light, and saw two girls by the lake. They were gazing dreamily at his reflection in the dark water. Bahloo became very self-conscious and hid behind a cloud.

'Bahloo makes everything look soft and silvery,' said one of the girls. 'He seems so kind and gentle.'

'He is so handsome,' said the other girl admiringly.

When Bahloo heard the compliments, he came out from behind the cloud. He shone brighter and stronger than ever. The compliments had given him a new confidence and he decided to descend to earth to meet the girls. Maybe one of them would marry him.

He stepped down to earth as lightly as the wind and walked through the bushes. He heard their voices, talking and laughing. It was like the sound of water running over stones. He sneaked up to where the voices came from. Through the tall reeds and bulrushes he saw the girls. One girl was lying on the sand, near the edge of the water. Her long hair streamed down over her shoulder. She was resting on one elbow. The other girl was sitting beside her. Bahloo parted the reeds, which rustled, and their laughter stopped. 'Hello!' he said cheerfully. The girls were blinded by his shining light and screamed in fear. They scrambled to their feet and began running towards their canoe.

'Wait for me,' pleaded Bahloo. 'Please don't run away from me.'

As Bahloo said that, he tripped on a rock and, stumbling, cried out in pain. The girls stopped on hearing his cry and turned to see if he needed help. Seeing them hesitate, Bahloo fell on his knees and begged them again. 'You are so beautiful. Please help me get up. I will not harm you.'

The girls exchanged glances. 'Perhaps we are too hard on him,' said one girl.

'Let's go back and help him.'

They walked over to Bahloo and helped him to his feet.

'Please take me across the lake,' asked Bahloo. He thought if he spent some time with the girls, they might change their minds about him. They took him to their canoe and asked him to sit in it.

'Only if you sit with me,' said Bahloo.

'You are so big and round. There is no room for us in the canoe. Now sit down and we'll tow you across,' said the girls. Bahloo sat down. The girls jumped into the water, caught the sides of the canoe in their hands and swam beside it, pulling the canoe across the lake. 'Come and live with me in the sky and I will make you very happy,' said Bahloo to the girls as they swam beside him. He could see the shoreline approaching and didn't have much time to win their hearts.

He decided they might like him better if he was a bit more playful. He reached over the side of the canoe and tickled one of the girls.

'Stop that or we'll scream for help,' said the girl, not amused by Moon's behaviour.

'And who will listen to your screams?' asked Bahloo wickedly. 'Nobody from your camp can hear you.'

The girls exchanged glances again and one of them dived under the canoe and joined her friend on the other side. They pulled the canoe with all their weight and tipped it over. With a scream, Bahloo sank into the water. He went deeper and deeper till only a sliver of his light could be seen at the bottom of the lake.

The girls got back in their canoe and hurried to their camp. They told the people of their tribe that Bahloo was dead. They had drowned him – he was at the bottom of the lake – and serve him right too.

Some of the elders were glad that Bahloo was dead. At least he would not annoy the young girls. But there were many who were alarmed at the prospect of having dark nights. 'Without Bahloo, our nights will be pitch black and dangerous. We will not be able to venture out at night at all,' they said.

They went to Wahn the Crow for advice.

'Bahloo the Moon is dead. What shall we do now? Will his spirit haunt us? Are we condemned to darkness forever?' they asked.

'Bahloo is not dead,' said Wahn the Crow, comforting the people. 'He is only hiding. He has nowhere to go except the empty spaces of the sky. But he is too embarrassed to come out. Slowly he will forget the shameful incident and he will appear again.' And Wahn the Crow was right. Bahloo the Moon, who had escaped from the lake and was back in the skies, came out again, peeping from behind the clouds, only a thin sliver at first, gradually growing bigger. As he became big and round he saw the maidens of earth by his own light. When he saw them, he remembered how he had been rejected by them and he began to shrink away in shame.

And so it has been since Dreamtime, and so it will be till the end of time.

# About the Stories

### The Greedy Man

In China, tales with moral themes served a purpose. Myths and stories taught proper behaviour by showing what happens to those who are immoral or arrogant. This myth from China was probably meant to instruct people in these cultural values and remind them that excessive greed is a dangerous trait to have in one's character.

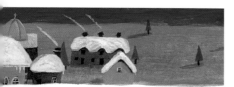

## The Thieves of Chelm

Chelm is a fabled town of fools in Eastern Europe. It is believed that when God wanted to fill the world with people, he sent two bags of souls to earth. One was filled with wise souls, the other with foolish, and they were supposed to be mixed up. But it so happened that the angel carrying the heavy bag of foolish souls, dropped it accidently while flying over the town of Chelm. The tales of Chelm are very popular in Jewish folklore and exist in many different versions.

## Anansi

Anansi is the trickster hero of his people. Although he is a spider, his characteristics are so human, that it is hard to imagine him just as an animal. Anansi's adventures are always about outsmarting adversaries and have delighted the people of West Africa, where the tales originated. These stories were later brought to the West Indies by the slaves.

## Hina

Hina myths are known throughout Polynesia in many different versions. Hina's struggle illustrates the human desire to break away and escape from the suffering of life.

# The Daughter of the Moon and the Son of the Sun

This tale comes from Siberia, probably the coldest and most forbidding place on earth. It explains the hostility between the two most important celestial bodies, the sun and the moon.

## The Rabbit and the Moon Man

Since human beings first looked up into the skies, they have wondered about the marks on the face of the moon. Beliefs about the rabbit in the moon are less prevalent than those about the man in the moon, but they exist in the Canadian Native, Chinese and Aztec moon lore.

## The Sun, Wind and the Moon

The source of this story is uncertain and it is difficult to locate it in time, because it has its roots in the oral tradition of storytelling in India. In a culture where obedience to elders is seen as a sacred trait, this tale from India glorifies the rewards of being obedient and considerate.

## The Buried Moon

Tales like these were reassuring to people who were often overwhelmed by the fear of the unknown. The story was first recorded in dialect in 1891.

## The Moon Princess

The myth of the Moon Princess takes place in ancient Japan where the supernatural was accepted as part of life.

## Why the Moon Waxes and Wanes

Most Aboriginal myths of Australia take place in Alchera or 'Dreamtime', believed to be a distant era when the ancestral spirits roamed the earth and taught people the art of survival.